# Puppy Mudge
# Finds a Friend

## By Cynthia Rylant

## Illustrated by Suçie Stevenson

READY-TO-READ

SIMON & SCHUSTER BOOKS FOR YOUNG READERS

New York   London   Toronto   Sydney

SIMON & SCHUSTER BOOKS FOR YOUNG READERS
An imprint of Simon & Schuster Children's Publishing Division
1230 Avenue of the Americas, New York, New York 10020
Text copyright © 2004 by Cynthia Rylant
Illustrations copyright © 2004 by Suçie Stevenson
All rights reserved, including the right of reproduction in whole or in part in any form.
SIMON & SCHUSTER BOOKS FOR YOUNG READERS is a trademark of Simon & Schuster, Inc.
READY-TO-READ is a registered trademark of Simon & Schuster, Inc.
Book design by Lucy Ruth Cummins
The text for this book is set in Goudy.
The illustrations for this book are rendered in pen-and-ink and watercolor.
Manufactured in the United States of America
10 9 8 7 6 5 4 3 2
CIP data for this book is available from the Library of Congress.
ISBN 978-0-689-83982-5

This is Puppy Mudge.
He lives with Henry.

# Mudge likes it.

He likes a lot of things.

# He likes chew toys.

# He likes crackers.

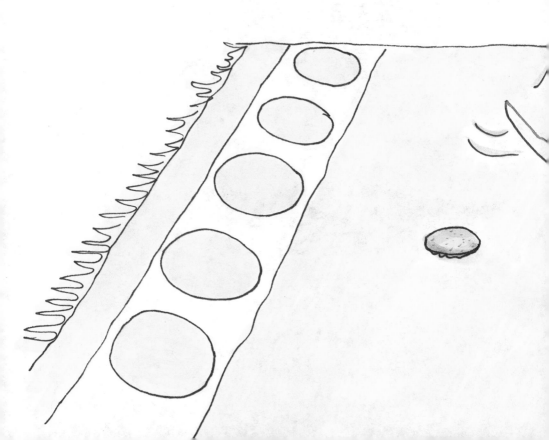

# He likes to drool.

(Mudge drools a lot.)

# Mudge also likes cats.

Mudge found a cat friend.

# Her name is Fluffy.

Mudge and Fluffy play.

**Fluffy runs.**

Mudge runs.

# Fluffy hides.

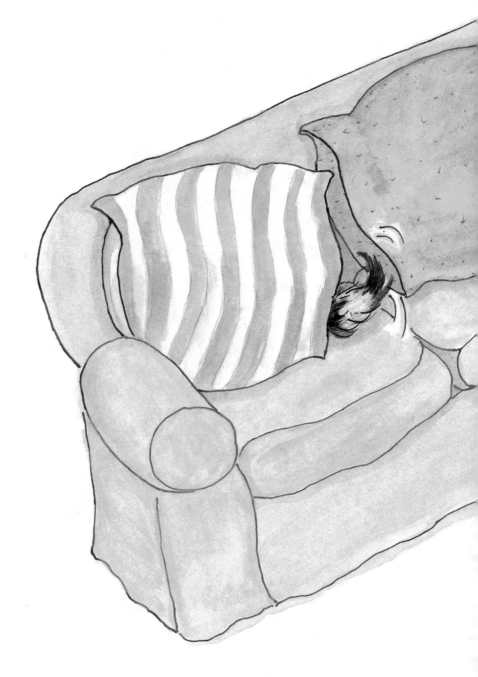

Mudge hides.

Fluffy climbs.

Mudge does not.

# Fluffy and Mudge play and play.

# Then they rest.

Fluffy purrs.
Mudge snores.

Friends.